Usborne
Forgotten Fairy Tales

Snow White
and Rose Red

Retold by Susanna Davidson

Illustrated by Isabella Grott

Reading consultant: Alison Kelly

About Forgotten Fairy Tales

People have been telling each other fairy tales for thousands of years. Then, a few hundred years ago, collectors began writing the stories down. The ones that became famous were the ones that reflected the ideas of the time.

These stories had patient, polite princesses such as *Snow White* and *Sleeping Beauty*. The tales with bold girls fighting their own battles were ignored.

This series brings to life the stories of those forgotten brave and brilliant girls...

Contents

Chapter 1

The two sisters

Once there were two sisters,
Snow White and Rose Red.

They were as different as
night and day. Rose Red
loved to climb trees. She was
as fast as a deer and as free
as a bird.

She dreamed of
adventure... of fighting
dragons or sailing the seas.

Snow White was happiest at home. She could weave baskets from rushes and carve creatures from wood.

Even though the sisters were so different, they loved each other very much. Together they cared for the garden and their beautiful rose trees.

In winter, they curled up by the fire and listened to their grandmother's stories.

One evening, as the snow fell thick and fast, there came a KNOCK! KNOCK! KNOCK! at the door.

"Quick!" said Grandmother. "Unlock the door. Someone must be out in the cold."

Rose Red sprang up and
unlocked the door. Only it
wasn't a person out in the
snow...

It was a bear!

Chapter 2

The bear

The bear was huge with thick fur and great white teeth. He peered into the room.

"Oh!" cried Rose Red, jumping back in surprise. Snow White darted behind her grandmother's chair.

"Don't be afraid," said the bear, in a deep, growly voice. "I won't hurt you. I'm just very, very cold..."

"Come and warm yourself by the fire," said Grandmother.

The bear dropped to all fours and lumbered into the cottage. *Crash!* went the table. Down fell the chairs.

He looked so gentle, Rose Red picked up the broom and began to brush the snow from his fur.

Snow White crept out from her hiding place and covered him with a blanket.

Grandmother went on with
her story. The bear curled up
by the fire and closed his eyes.

Soon, the cottage was filled
with the sound of the bear's
rumbling snores.

The next morning, Snow White opened the door and the bear lolloped away into the forest. After that, he came all through the winter...

...and into spring.

Snow White
and Rose Red
rode on his
back...

...stroked the soft fur
on his tummy...

...and
tickled his
whiskery nose.

18

The girls longed to know the bear's secret. But they didn't dare ask.

19

Then, one morning, the bear turned to the girls. His dark eyes were full of sadness. "Summer is coming," he said. "It's time for me to go."

Oh! Please don't leave!

"I'm under a curse," said
the bear. "Long ago, a wicked
creature stole something
precious from me."

I must return
to the forest
to find it.

But as the bear hurried out, his
coat caught on the door... and
tore. Rose Red thought she saw
shining gold beneath his fur.

Before she could look again, the bear had gone, heading deeper into the forest.

I wonder if we'll ever see him again...

Chapter 3

The ungrateful goblin

The blossom fell from the trees.
The roses opened their petals.
It was summer at last.

They all missed the bear, but Snow White missed him most of all. "He might be in trouble. I'd do anything to help him."

"Then let's go into the forest and find him," said Rose Red.

So the sisters packed
their bags and kissed their
grandmother goodbye.

Take care!
Stay together.

They hadn't gone far,
when they heard a strange
squawking noise.
There, on the path
ahead...

...was a goblin. He was
jumping up and down, trying
to free his beard from a branch.

"Don't just stand there!"
shouted the goblin.

"Of course we'll help," said
Rose Red, and she reached into
her pocket for her scissors.

With a SNIP! SNIP! SNIP!
of the scissors, the goblin
was free.

"How dare you cut off my
beard?" snarled the goblin.
"The end was the best part!"

He snatched up his bag and
Rose Red saw it was full of
sparkling jewels.

"What are you looking at?" snarled the goblin. He swung the bag over his shoulder and hurried away.

Rose Red sighed. "He didn't even say thank you!"

Chapter 4

The bear's return

That night, the sisters slept in the forest. The next morning, they headed down to the river, to catch a fish for breakfast.

There was the goblin again.
"My beard is tangled in these
thorns," he shouted. "Help me!"
SNIP! SNIP! SNIP! went
Rose Red's scissors.

"Fools!" screamed the goblin, his face red with rage. "How dare you cut my beard."

He grabbed his sack, shining with pearls, and strode away.

"Ruder and ruder," said Rose Red, watching him go.

The sisters slept deep in the forest that night.

In the morning, they set off to search for their bear once more.

They crossed a bridge and came to a clearing in the trees.

There, circling above them,
was an eagle.

It made a sudden swoop
to the ground. Then came a
sharp, piercing cry. Rose Red
and Snow White ran towards
the sound...

...and found the goblin, caught in the eagle's claws.

Help me!

"This eagle is going to fly away with me," shouted the goblin. "Do something!"

Both girls leaped up
and grabbed the goblin's feet,
clinging on tight. At last, the
eagle let go...

...and they tumbled to the
ground in a heap.

"You're so clumsy!" snapped
the goblin. "You should be
more careful."

He reached for his bulging
sack and Rose Red saw a glint
of gold.

As the goblin turned
to go, they heard a shout.
Looking up, they saw the
bear in the distance.

"That's the thief!" cried the
bear. "Stop him!"

Chapter 5

The golden cloak

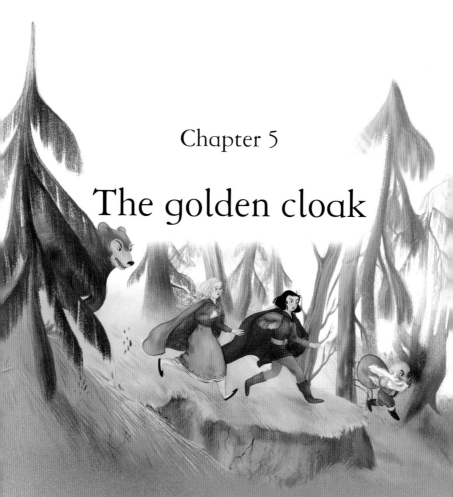

They all raced after the
goblin. Rose Red reached him
first. She grabbed the goblin's
beard and held fast.

Then the bear raised his paws. "Give me back my treasure!" he growled.

"It's in the b-b-bag," stammered the goblin, trembling with fear.

The bear tore open the bag.
Out spilled shining pearls,
sparkling jewels... and a
golden cloak.

The bear flung the cloak
over his back. In a blinding
flash of light, there stood a
dazzling prince.

The goblin let out a cry.

"Go away and never come back!" ordered the prince.

The goblin fled.

Then the prince turned to the sisters. "Thank you," he said. "You and your grandmother kept me warm through the winter, and now you've helped me break the goblin's curse."

From that day on, the
sisters often visited the prince
at his palace.

In time, Snow White and the
prince fell deeply in love, and
were married.

As for Rose Red – she roams
the world still, living a life
of adventure...

About the story

Snow White and Rose Red is a German fairy tale. It was first written down by Caroline Stahl, in 1818, in her collection of German fairy tales. She called the tale *The Ungrateful Dwarf.*

Then two brothers, Jacob and Wilhelm Grimm, included the story in their book of fairy tales, renaming it *Snow White and Rose Red.*

It's unusual for a fairy tale, as it's about two sisters who love and help each other. In this version, there is also a new ending, to reflect the times we live in.

Designed by Samantha Barrett
Series designer: Russell Punter
Series editor: Lesley Sims
Digital manipulation:
John Russell and Nick Wakeford

First published in 2020 by Usborne Publishing Ltd.,
Usborne House, 83-85 Saffron Hill, London EC1N 8RT, England.
usborne.com Copyright © 2020, 2019 Usborne Publishing Ltd.